Crazy Pizza Day

Written by **Bonnie Dobkin**
Illustrated by **Romi Dey**

TeachingStrategies™ • Washington D.C.

For Teaching Strategies, Inc.
Publisher: Larry Bram
Editorial Director: Hilary Parrish Nelson
VP Curriculum and Assessment: Cate Heroman
Product Manager: Kai-leé Berke
Book Development Team: Sherrie Rudick and Jan Greenberg
Project Manager: Jo A. Wilson

For Q2AMedia
Editorial Director: Bonnie Dobkin
Editor and Curriculum Adviser: Suzanne Barchers
Program Manager: Gayatri Singh
Creative Director: Simmi Sikka
Project Manager: Santosh Vasudevan
Illustrator: Romi Dey
Designer: Neha Kaul

Teaching Strategies, Inc.
P.O. Box 42243
Washington, DC 20015
www.TeachingStrategies.com

ISBN: 978-1-60617-150-9

Library of Congress Cataloging-in-Publication Data
Dobkin, Bonnie.
  Crazy Pizza Day/ written by Bonnie Dobkin ; illustrated by Romi Dey.
    p. cm.
  Summary: On Crazy Pizza Day, when a restaurant decides to offer any topping the customer wants, some of the requests are surprising.
  ISBN 978-1-60617-150-9
 [1. Stories in rhyme. 2. Pizza--Fiction. 3. Restaurants--Fiction. 4. Humorous stories.]
  I. Dey, Romi, ill. II. Title.
  PZ8.3.D634Cr 2010
  [E]--dc22
                                    2009036781

CPSIA tracking label information:
RR Donnelley, Shenzhen, China
Date of Production: March 2012
Cohort: Batch 2

Printed and bound in China

3 4 5 6 7 8 9 10	15 14 13 12
Printing	Year Printed

CRAZY PIZZA DAY

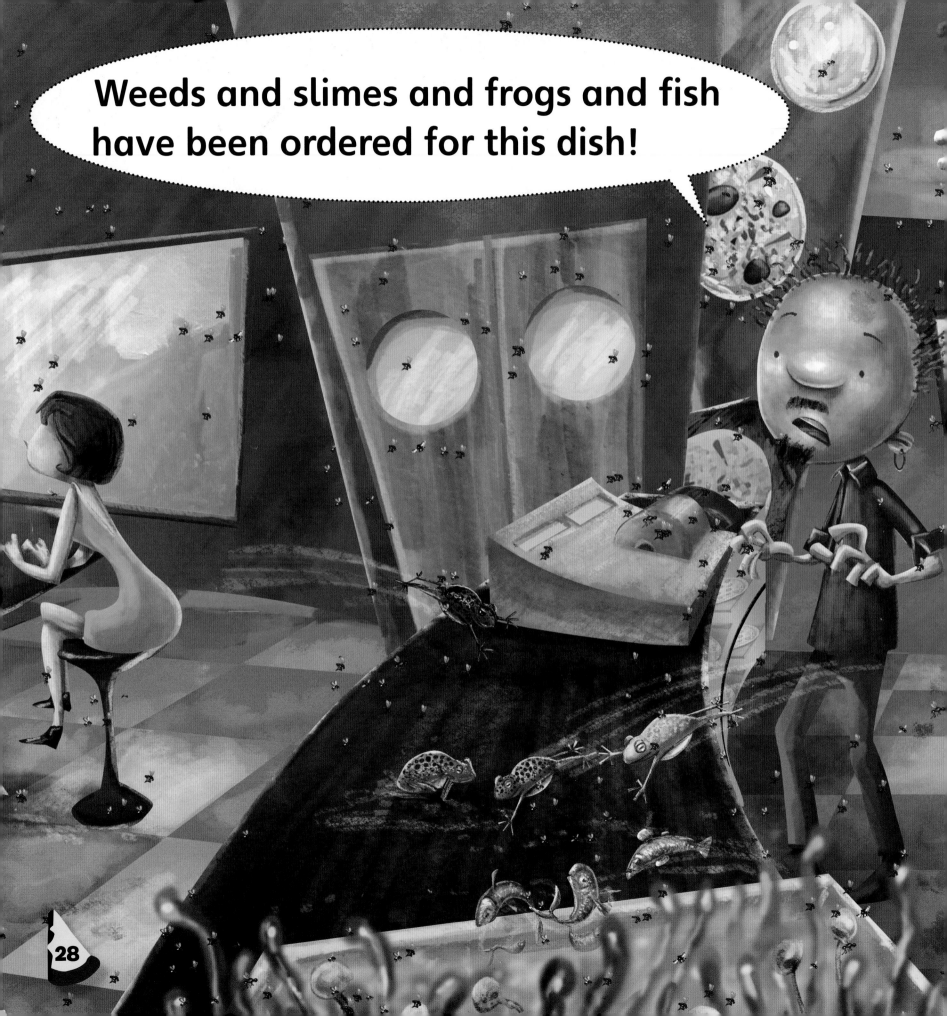